Dear Jason,

I hope these stones become part of your story. May you con't living in faith and part of God's story.

Peace&love

Vicki
3-31-07

Camdyn

Presented to:

_____

Given by:

_____

Date:

_____

Occasion:

Coyote
Meets
Jesus

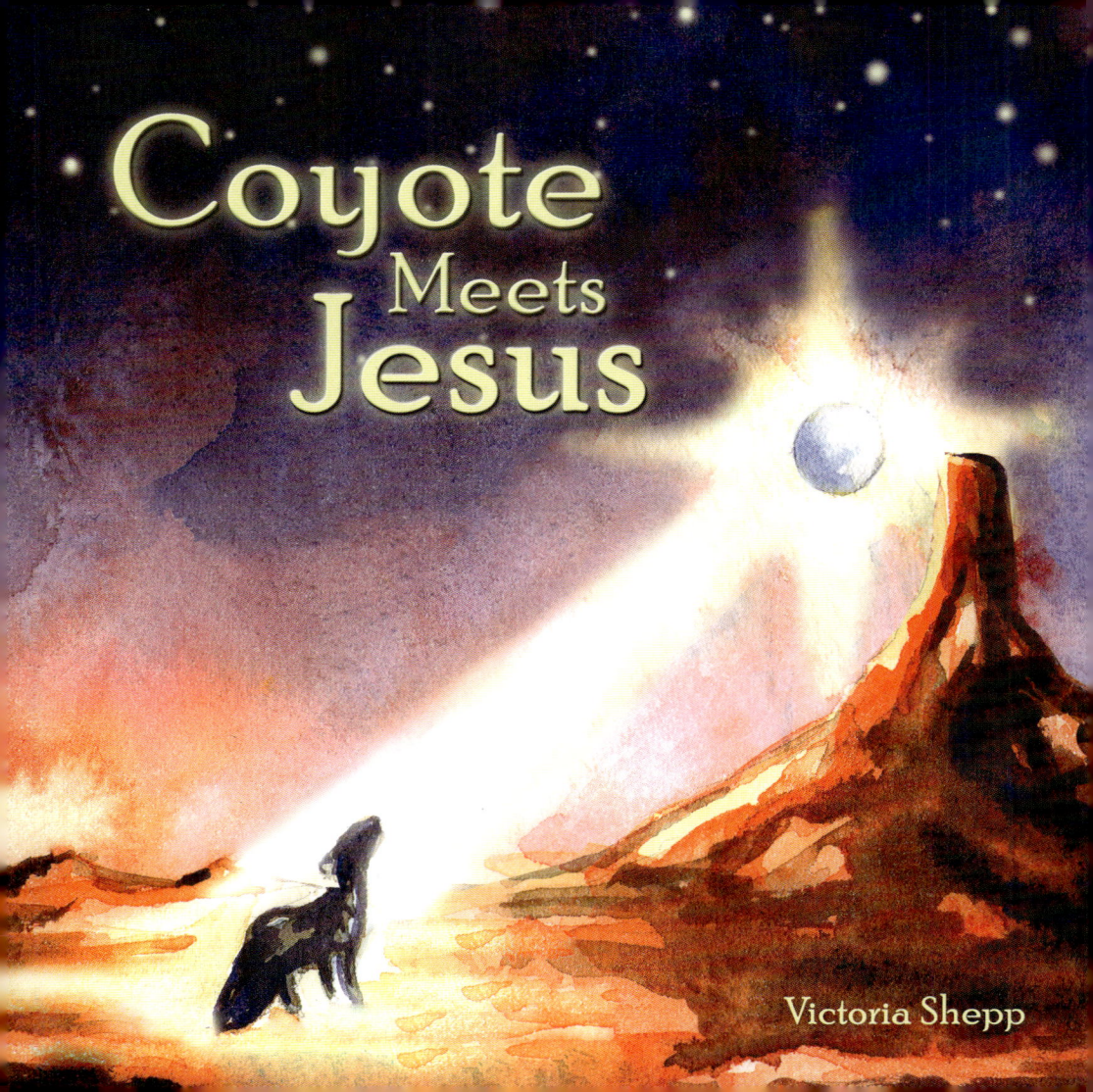

Victoria Shepp

Coyote Meets Jesus

Treasures in Folktales and Scripture

Saint Mary's Press®

Victoria Shepp

Genuine recycled paper with 10% post-consumer waste. 5106600

The publishing team included Virginia Halbur, development editor; Lorraine Kilmartin, reviewer; prepress and manufacturing coordinated by the prepublication and production services departments of Saint Mary's Press.

Cover and interior illustrations by Eric Lervold, Pernsteiner Creative Group. www.pernsteiner.com

Printed in Canada

Printing: 9 8 7 6 5 4 3 2 1

Year: 2014 13 12 11 10 09 08 07 06

ISBN-13: 978-0-88489-889-4
ISBN-10: 0-88489-889-X

Library of Congress Cataloging-in-Publication Data

Shepp, Victoria.
    Coyote meets Jesus : treasures in folktales and Scripture / Victoria Shepp .
    p. cm.
ISBN 0-88489-889-X (hardbound)
    1. Catholic youth—Religious life. 2. Tales. 3. Christian life—Biblical teaching. 4. Bible. N.T.—Criticism, interpretation, etc. I. Title.
BX2355.S55 2006
242'.63—dc22

                                    2005027063

Dedication

This book is dedicated to those who have blessed me by allowing me to be a part of their story.

Author's Acknowledgments

You would not be holding this book if it were not for a number of people. Although I cannot list them all, I would like to thank my editor, Ginny Halbur, for all of her input, encouragement, and creativity. We have not only created a book together, but a friendship as well. I also want to thank my sounding board, draft reader, and best friend, Paulette Smith, for listening to and reading these tales over and over. These stories are richer because of her patience and wisdom. Last but not least, I would like to thank my parents for opening up the world of stories to me at an early age. Peace and love to you all!

Contents

Introduction

*C*oyote Meets Jesus sounds like the beginning line of a joke, but the title of this book is inspired by a character that is central to many Native American folktales. Coyote, sometimes known as Mr. or Dr. Coyote, is a trickster, a fall guy, a wise one, a student, and a teacher. He is both the mischief maker and the hero. Coyote was chosen as the title character of this book because he represents both the good and bad that are characteristic of human nature.

Folktales are oral, mythic stories that use elements from nature and human experience to convey the beliefs, fears, values, and hopes shared by people of every age and culture. Jesus also used elements from nature and human experience in his stories and teachings to convey God's grand plan for creation. Comparing Jesus's stories with folktales from different cultures can be fun and inspirational.

Storytelling and the Bible

Nearly every culture uses storytelling as entertainment and as a teaching tool. From African villages to the Pacific Rim, from freezing Alaska to tropical Brazil, stories are told and retold. Many different types of stories entice the listener—fairy tales, legends, sagas, anecdotes, explanatory tales, fables, and more. These stories, which were often refashioned over time, were told to pass down the history and tradition of the people and places where the stories originated. Some stories crossed cultural boundaries and were adopted by other peoples. The messages in the stories were often universal and tried to provide answers to some of life's most difficult questions.

Sacred Scripture is also a collection of different types of literature—historical accounts, poetic and symbolic writings, prophecies, and mythic tales that attempt to answer the great questions of how we came to be and of our purpose in life. The various stories in the Bible record the events in the life of God's people. Each story is written in a style that best conveys the message of our faith. The sacred writings, inspired by the Holy Spirit, are woven together to form the Judeo-Christian Scriptures— the great story of God's love for humankind!

13

This book examines universal themes found in folk-tales—greed and generosity, revenge and forgiveness, despair and hope—and compares and contrasts those themes with Jesus's teachings in Scripture. It is hoped that by seeing the similarities and differences in the Scriptures and folktales, you, the reader, will be able to see that different people, from different times and places, have similar questions about life and how to live it. These stories are intended to not only challenge you to experience different cultures but also to see, think, and even act differently.

Ideas for Using This Book

Each chapter in this book begins with a folktale from a different culture. As you read the folktales, imagine the characters, their voices, and their facial expressions. Put yourself in their place and think about how you would react. The folktales are then followed by Jesus's story, which begins with a Scripture citation that you will need to look up in a Bible. Use your imagination as you read the Scripture passage in the same way that you read the folktale. As you do so, give some thought to how your own life story is reflected in Jesus's story. These Scripture stories may be familiar to you, but even if you have heard them before, you may hear something new. The story may not have changed, but you have been changed by time, experience, and by the story itself.

After reading the Scripture story, read the reflection that follows. It compares common themes in the folktale and the Scripture passage and then connects those themes to our everyday lives. Even though many of these folktales originate in non-Christian cultures, the messages contained in them could easily have been conveyed in Christ's parables. The folktales are fictional and sometimes even fantastic stories, but they can offer new perspectives on life's dilemmas. The Scriptures take us a step further by teaching us "what God wants us to know for [our] salvation" (*The Catholic Faith Handbook*, p. 28).

The outcomes of these folktales vary, just like the outcomes in stories from Scripture. Some people may accept the "happily ever after" ending, but just as many ask, "Now what?" One thing we do know from Scripture is that God is present—then, now, and into the future. As each story ends, it is really just a beginning. This question remains: How do you continue to tell God's story through your life? God doesn't promise us "happily ever after," and neither do the folktales. However, God does promise to be with us in this life and in the life hereafter. The end of each chapter features questions that will help you answer, "Now what?" This is your chance to take what you've learned from the folktales and Scriptures and put it into action in your life. Reading about forgiving one's brother or sister is great, but living out forgiveness in one's family is how one lives as a disciple of Jesus Christ. Jesus sets an example for us through the stories he tells and through the actions of his life, death, and Resurrection. It is now your turn to continue the story through the actions of your life.

A Dream, a Journey, and a Treasure

(England)

He was just a simple man living in a simple English cottage. William was his name, and he lived and worked and prayed and did his best. The cottage was located in the village of Swingham, England. It had a little kitchen, a little bed, and a little place for him to sit and read. In the village, some people had all they needed, and others needed a hand. William's family and friends thought he was nice and funny and good. William even thought he was nice and funny and good. But William also knew there was something missing. He wanted to do more to help others and to be generous. William worked long and hard and didn't have a lot of time or money to donate to charity. But something happened to change all of that.

For three nights in a row, William woke with a start, remembering his dream. It was a vivid dream, and he remembered every detail. Each night he would recall another part of the dream. The first night he remembered going to London. He remembered the city and everything about it, even though he had never visited it. And it wasn't just because he had seen pictures of London in the newspaper. It was as if he had really visited. William realized he was going to London for a good reason, but he didn't really know why, so he returned to his slumber. The second night William remembered going to London just like the first night. This night, however, he remembered the double-decker bus he rode in and the exact park he walked in. He remembered seeing the street signs, the curves of the park's paths, the little pond, and the kiddie playground. William still didn't know exactly why he was dreaming this way, so he returned to sleep. The third night he recalled the city, the double-decker bus, the park, and something new. He remembered that there was a treasure buried under a particular bench in the park. This night William got up instead of returning to sleep. He said to himself, "I need to go to London, get on that double-decker bus, go to that particular park, and find that bench. There I will find the treasure and become rich so that I can help more people!"

William packed his belongings in a little knapsack and left his simple English cottage. As he left town, his friends asked where he was headed. "I am going to London to find the treasure," he would answer, and his friends would stare at him open-jawed. But that didn't stop William, although he did have some misgivings. A little out of town he thought about going back, but, sure of his dream, he pressed on. It took awhile to reach London, but once there William boarded the double-decker bus that circled the city. He saw the park from the top of the bus and pulled the cord that signaled the driver to stop. As he entered the park, he saw the bench from his dreams. William stared at the bench and realized there was no way he could dig under the cement the bench was sitting on. He was saddened and sat dejectedly on the bench. As he did so, the park warden sat next to him. "What are you doing?" the warden asked.

"I came for a treasure but see it is impossible to obtain," said William.

"Why did you think you would find a treasure here?" asked the warden. William told him about his dream and the warden laughed. "Silly man, I had a dream for more than three nights myself. But in my dream I was supposed to go to the village of Swingham and find a man named William. When I found him, I was to buy his home and find a treasure buried under the front step."

He laughed again, "Do you see me traveling all of the way to Swingham? Ha!"

William looked at the man and shook his head. Slowly he left the park and made his way back to his little village. As he arrived, his friends asked if he had found the treasure. William didn't answer; he just plodded along until he got to his little cottage. He looked at that front step and saw for the first time the patch of earth under it. He ran to his shed, got a shovel, and started digging. William unearthed a treasure that was so great he was able to live comfortably and take care of the people of his village.

Jesus's Story (Matthew 25:14-30)

God gives treasures to each one of us. Those treasures may not be magnificent chests filled with coins and jewels, but God's gifts are present in each one of us. The gifts and opportunities God gives us are meant to grow and be shared. Jesus tells a story called the parable of the talents, in which three slaves are given talents (a measure of money). Two of the slaves double the amount of money for their owner, and the other just hides his, afraid of what might happen if he loses it or the investment doesn't pay off.

In the folktale William is like one of the slaves who used his talents wisely. William could have ignored the opportunity he was presented with, stayed safely at home, and continued to keep his treasure buried. However, he chose to take a risk, follow his dream, and travel all the way to London. It is sometimes risky to follow our dreams and use our talents, but that is what God wants of us. In the parable the slaves who risked everything by investing the talents given to them were rewarded and called trustworthy. The slave who was so afraid of losing what he had took no risks and just buried his talents. He wound up losing not only the little he had but also an unexpected reward at the end. The warden in the folktale is even more skeptical than the slave who hid his talents. His dream is not in finding his own treasure but that of another, and even then he scoffs at the possibility. In the end it is William, not the warden, who is rewarded for his search. He discovers that his treasure was under his own doorstep all along.

We all have opportunities to discover and use the gifts that God has given to us—whether it is the ability to play a musical instrument, solve a difficult math problem, hit a home run, or share our wealth. Each of us is called to discover our gifts, develop them, and use them for the good of others. If we are like the warden who wants what belongs to another or like the slave who buries his talents, then we are sure to lose all that we have been given. But if we are like William and the wise slaves who not only recognize their treasures and talents but also use them wisely to help others, then in the end we will find the real treasure—eternal life in the Kingdom of God.

What gifts or talents have I been given? How do I use them for the good of others?

Coyote and the Monster

(Native American)

Coyote was quite furry and had a wet nose, most of the time. As a desert creature, he knew his way around the canyons and plateaus. Because Coyote was so well known, many stories are told of him. This is one.

The sun was out. Being early spring, it was dry and warm, but not stifling hot like summer. Coyote lumbered along the well-worn path, sniffing the

brush and occasionally jumping to catch, or trying to catch, the small flies that buzzed in front of him on the path. Coyote hadn't seen his friend White Beard in a long time, and he wondered how the old goat was doing. He and White Beard always had fun, sometimes even playing practical jokes at their own expense. Coyote mused that it had also been a long time since he and Puma had shared a laugh, and even longer since Donkey had spoken to him. Coyote continued on the path, hoping to run into one of his friends, but he didn't see anyone—not even smelly Skunk or itchy Tick. Coyote couldn't figure out where all his friends were hiding. As it was, the shadows began to grow, the day cooled, and his stomach growled—all signals to the end of the day and the start of dinnertime.

Dinnertime was so much fun with his friends; they would sit around the fire and tell stories. He and his friends knew all of the stories of creation and told them to the young animals when they were around. They also knew stories that were told just for fun and would tell those when they wanted a few laughs. Coyote was hoping to find some of his friends so they could share a meal and a story.

Coyote continued on his way until he heard a loud noise. Looking up, he saw a cave and heard a rumbling noise echoing out of it. Coyote thought he heard the voices of his friends among the rumbling. Carefully Coyote entered the dark, damp, and noisy cavern. Coyote walked a long way and came upon Puma lying on the ground, panting and looking tired. "Puma, what is wrong?" Coyote asked. "Food, hungry, starving," was all that ravenous Puma could say. Coyote told Puma to wait while he went for food. He walked further into the cave but did not see any tender cacti or even a tuft of grass.

Coyote then came upon White Beard, who also looked frail, tired, and hungry. "White Beard, you always find something to eat, what is going on? Why are you and Puma so hungry?" Coyote was getting quite concerned. White Beard told Coyote that they were all trapped in the belly of a monster and that they were starving to death. "No, you're wrong," Coyote answered, "I walked into a cave and found you here. This isn't a monster!" White Beard turned and pointed to Tick, Donkey, and Skunk, who were standing right behind him. They also were starving, tired, and miserable. The old goat told Coyote that the cave Coyote thought he had walked into was actually the mouth of the monster, and that he too would starve. Although White Beard often played tricks on him, once Coyote touched the sides of the cave and decided it was flesh, and smelled the rotten breath of the monster that he first thought was the wind, Coyote realized that they really were inside a monster.

Coyote was now anxious to save his friends. Coyote was smart; he knew that the best meat was all around them, so he started pulling belly fat from the sides of the monster. After Coyote fed his friends, they all looked much better. His friends thanked him, but they were still concerned for their safety. They asked Coyote how they were going to escape. Coyote had a plan. He would find the monster's heart and kill him. All agreed that it was a fine plan. Coyote walked around the belly of the monster listening for its heartbeat. When he found it, he began to tear at it. Monster yelled at his belly, "Stop that! It hurts; don't bother my heart!" Coyote continued until the monster coughed, at which time Coyote and all his friends flew from the monster's belly out onto the ground. The last one out nearly got caught in the monster's teeth. Although he was flat from sliding through the monster's mouth, Tick was happy he was alive, and celebrated with all the other creatures.

Jesus's Story (Matthew 14:13-21)

Coyote loved his friends. He liked to spend time with them, tell stories with them, and have fun with them. Coyote was distressed when he found his friends starving to death in what he thought was a cave. He did everything he could to help them. Jesus was like that too; he loved his friends. He spent time with them, told them stories, and didn't want to see them starve—physically or spiritually.

Once a huge crowd of five thousand people were following Jesus because of his teachings and wisdom. Like Coyote, Jesus noticed that many of them suffered, and he wanted to help them. It was late in the day, and the people began to grow hungry. Knowing they were far from any town, Jesus did not want to send the crowd away hungry, so he told his disciples to feed them. But, like Coyote's friends, the problem seemed too big for the disciples to solve. They wanted to send everyone away. Jesus, however, knew that the people's hunger was much deeper than their physical hunger. The people needed his help to survive.

Just as Coyote came up with a clever plan to help his friends, Jesus also came up with a clever plan to meet the needs of all God's people. Jesus told the disciples to bring to him the food that was available—five loaves and two fish. After Jesus blessed and broke the bread, he told the disciples to feed the crowd. Amazingly, everyone ate and there was plenty left over.

Jesus's plan really calls all of us to share what we have, no matter how little, in order to help others. The sacrifices we make for others add up and multiply. What seems impossible is all of a sudden possible. In breaking the bread and feeding the five thousand people, Jesus gives us a glimpse into his Last Supper and his own sacrifice on the cross to save us all. Jesus's plan establishes God's Kingdom on earth.

Coyote cared for his friends, and Jesus cares for us even more. Jesus wants both our physical needs (like having enough food) and our spiritual needs met. It was not enough that Coyote fed his friends; he also helped them get out of the monster's belly. Coyote was a hero to those he saved. Jesus is our hero as well, and his plan isn't just that we have enough to eat; it is that we have the promise of eternal life in the Kingdom of God. Jesus shows us that our life in the Kingdom begins right now, and that through our sacrifices—blessed, broken, and added to his in the Eucharist—we are able to meet the needs of the world, with plenty left over. Even clever Mister Coyote couldn't beat that!

How am I helping to make the Kingdom of God happen here and now?

The Brothers' Fortune

(Korea)

They were brothers: two grown men from the same family, and yet they were very different. Joo~chan, the younger brother, was kind, considerate, and well liked. However, he was not lucky and was very poor. He tried hard, worked long hours, and did everything he could, but his little family was often left hungry. It was late one day when Joo~chan returned from working the fields. As he neared his simple home, a commotion erupted in the brush next to the path. A snake had slithered up a tree and was busy devouring a nest full of birds. As he shooed the snake away, he heard a little peep and saw that one of the baby birds was caught in the brush. He lifted the baby bird from the bamboo and noticed that it had an injured wing. Joo-chan took the little bird home, where he and his family tended it. Once the little bird was better, it flew south with the other birds. The whole family, especially Joo-chan, was sorry to see it go but pleased that it had recovered so well.

The seasons changed, and birds began flying back to Joo-chan's tiny village in Korea. Joo-chan watched the birds overhead and noticed one drop a seed right in front of him, right into his tiny vegetable patch. Joo-chan watered the seed and waited. Very quickly, within days, it began to sprout, and soon large gourds had blossomed on the vine. Joo-chan and his family were amazed and decided that they should open the gourds. Ceremoniously they cut open the first gourd, and out of it poured rice. The little family shouted with joy; it was more rice than they had seen in a long time. Quickly they opened the next gourd, and out of it spilled gold coins. Again the family shouted with joy. Now Joo-chan was able to take good care of his family, and they never went hungry again.

Meanwhile, Joo-chan's older brother got more and more angry. Seung was not a nice man, was never a good brother, and couldn't believe that Joo-chan had gotten so lucky. Even though Seung had all he needed, he demanded to know what Joo-chan had done. Joo-chan, knowing that he needed to honor his older brother, told him about the snake and the little bird he rescued. He told him how he mended the bird's wing and took care of it until it flew south. Then he told him about the gourds, the rice, and the gold. Seung left his brother in a hurry, plotting his own path to greater riches.

Once home, Seung lured a little bird into his yard, where she built a nest. Soon her tiny eggs hatched. A few days later, Seung made one of the babies fall out of the nest. Seung injured its leg and then cared for it, fixing it and waiting for the time when it would fly south. For Seung, spring couldn't come soon enough. When it did come, and the birds began flying back to their village, Seung saw his little bird fly over and drop a seed in the plot near his house. Greedily he planted the seed and waited. Just as in Joo-chan's case, the gourds came up quickly and were larger than normal. Seung hurriedly split open the first gourd and out came little scamps, who beat him with their little sticks, saying, "We will beat you for being so mean and greedy." Because they were so small, he took the beating. After that they disappeared. Seung still believed that the next gourd would contain gold, so he opened it. Out of it came fifty debt collectors, demanding that Seung repay all that he had borrowed, swindled, and stolen over the years. He gave them everything, still convinced that the next gourd would hold riches. After paying off all his loans, he split open the third gourd, and from it came not gold, but a flood that covered his only remaining asset—his house.

Wet and unhappy, poor and humiliated, Seung, sorry
for what he had done, went to his brother's house and
told his own story. Joo-chan, still the considerate
younger brother, took in Seung. Joo-chan accepted
Seung's apology and shared his wealth with his brother.
They lived together in peace and happiness from that
day on.

Jesus's Story (Luke 15:11-32)

One of Jesus's parables, well known as the parable of the
prodigal son, is also a story about two brothers who
experience greed, jealousy, and ultimately forgiveness.
A prodigal is a person who either spends or gives lavishly. In Jesus's parable the younger son is generous with his
father's wealth. But unlike Joo-chan, the younger son

spends it on himself. The story begins with the younger son demanding his share of the family property, intended as his inheritance when his father dies. After the father divides his property between the two sons, the younger son takes his share, leaves home, and foolishly spends it all. This younger son is the "prodigal" because he lavishly spends his father's wealth on luxuriant living—indulging his selfish desires. Remorseful and penniless, the younger son finally returns to his father and asks for his forgiveness. The father not only runs out to welcome his youngest son home but also throws him a grand party to celebrate his return. The father can also be viewed as prodigal because he lavishly gives the younger son all that he wants and more.

Now the older son—who had stayed home, worked hard on the family farm, and did everything he was asked—is furious at his father's generosity. His greed for his father's love and affection leads to jealousy and resentment of his father's love and forgiveness toward his younger brother upon his return. He does not understand that his father's abundant love is equally available to both of them.

In the Korean folktale, Seung (the older brother) loses all his possessions because of his heartlessness, greed, and jealousy. In the parable, the older brother's jealousy and greed prevent him from seeing that he possesses something greater than material wealth—his father's love. Like the prodigal father, Joo-chan (the younger son) is faced with a choice—he can either forgive his brother and welcome him back with open arms, or he can refuse to accept Seung's apology and let him suffer even more for his actions. It must have been very difficult for Joo-chan to forgive Seung after so many years of unkindness, but, because of Joo-chan's forgiveness and kindness, in the end the two brothers live together in mutual peace and happiness.

Jesus used parables, as well as his actions, to teach us the importance of forgiveness. God is the prodigal father who lavishly and generously forgives us when we repent and ask God's forgiveness—no matter what our sins. God is also calling us to be generous with our love and to forgive others—especially our own family members. And even though forgiving someone is sometimes the hardest thing to do, it can also be the most rewarding.

How can I be more generous and forgiving in my relationships with siblings, other family members, and friends?

47

How Daya Got Her Sari

(India)

She was a good daughter, and he was a caring father. Simple and poor, but happy, Daya and her father lived peacefully in their little village in northern India. They made do with the little they had, and luckily there were sisam trees near their village. Daya's father was able to use sisam wood to create fanciful carvings, which he sold each week at the market. Daya usually stayed at home to take care of their little home. Daya's father appreciated all she did and treated her very well. Each week he said, "Come with me, Daughter. Walk with me to the market and wander the stalls." Every week she said no because she only had one sari and was embarrassed; it was old, worn, and drab. After she replied in her usual manner, "No, thank you, Father, I will stay home," he asked a new question. This time he asked, "What can I bring home for you, Daya?" Normally Daya would have said nothing, but this week their poverty stung at her, and she told her father that she would like a new sari. Then just as quickly she changed her mind, "No, Father, I really don't need one. Bring me a little flour, and I will make you a great meal."

Going off to the market without her, Daya's father sold all his carvings—even the most fanciful and exotic.

When he was done, he counted his earnings—not even enough for a length of fabric, let alone a sari. Daya's father was very sad as he bought the flour. He wished he could buy a beautiful sari for his only child.

When Daya's father returned home, he gave his daughter the flour, but told Daya that he was leaving to dine with friends for the evening meal. Because Daya's recipe for naan made enough for two, that is what she made, knowing she'd have enough for a second helping. As she turned from her cookstove, she saw a stranger carrying a beautiful bouquet of flowers and struggling to make his way on the path. He looked famished, and the flowers were a stark contrast to his drab, downtrodden appearance. Daya looked at the stranger and then at the naan she carried. As much as she would have liked another serving, Daya gave the flat bread to him. He looked at her in thanks, nibbled on the naan, and then presented her with the bouquet. The stranger walked away eating the naan, seeming to gain strength as he did so. Daya gazed at the flowers, inhaled their fragrance, and began walking to the river to acquire water to place them in.

As she walked to the river, Daya met a man who was carrying two pots. He was struggling to carry them both, as they were a little large. "Sir, is there a way I can help?" Daya asked, hands together in greeting. "I am a pot maker and sold many today at market. I was coming home, when thieves stole my cart, breaking the pots as they laughed and rode away. I was only able to save these two. My wife will be very worried about me, and I have a long way to go." Daya, looking at her beautiful bouquet, turned to the man and said, "Here, take these flowers. Your wife will like them, I'm sure." She arranged the flowers in one of the pots and began to walk away. "Wait!" he said, "Take this other pot; I cannot carry it all the way home, and you have been very sympathetic to me." Daya took the pot and continued walking toward the river, thinking she'd fill the pot and water her little garden at home. When Daya got to the riverside, she came upon an old woman who, bent over a stone on the river, was trying to do some wash. Not too far away from the woman sat a broken pot. Daya, knowing how much easier it would be to do the wash in the pot, offered it to the old woman, who gratefully accepted it. Before Daya was too far away, the woman cried out to her, "Please, take this." Daya saw the woman holding up the most beautiful sari. She couldn't believe it! Daya gently took the sari from the old woman who said, "It was mine when I was your age. Now it is yours, in thanks for your kindness."

Jesus's Story (Matthew 7:7-12)

God, like Daya's father, wants us to have what we need and wants us to be happy. In chapters 5 through 7 of Matthew's Gospel, Jesus shares a series of teachings with his disciples that are known as the Sermon on the Mount. Jesus's teachings, beginning with the Beatitudes, are filled with challenging new ideas—both for those living in Jesus's time and for us today. In the Sermon on the Mount, Jesus tells his followers to, "Ask, and it will be given you; search, and you will find; knock, and the door will be opened for you" (Mt 7:7). Jesus isn't talking about asking for every piece of trendy clothing or new video game that comes along, but for those things that will aid our spiritual, physical, and emotional well-being. And, as much as God wants us to have good things, we are also expected to add to the good of the world by our actions: "In everything do to others as you would have them do to you; for this is the law and the prophets" (Mt 7:12).

In the folktale, Daya made wise decisions that helped the people she encountered as well as herself. Through her generosity she not only added to the good of those around her but also ultimately got what she wanted—although that was not Daya's motivation for helping others.

We can't presume that God does not hear our prayer or does not care about us just because we don't get *everything* we desire or because bad things come our way. Daya's father did what he could with the little he had; he couldn't buy Daya a sari, but he did give her flour. You may ask for one thing and not realize that what you have been given may be enough, even though it may not seem like enough or like an answer to your prayer at the time. If Daya had thought that way and not shared what she had been given, the people she encountered would not have been helped. Daya's generosity and kindness proved that small acts of kindness can produce blessings beyond our imagination— flour can be turned into a sari.

Our faith story is full of people who asked God for help in times of need. It is also filled with stories of people who sacrificed the little they had to help others.

Many of these people, like Daya, helped others just because they knew it was right, not because they thought they'd get a reward. God wants us to ask, seek, and knock for all our needs, but God also expects us to be kind and help others in need. Jesus tells us, in the Sermon on the Mount and throughout the Gospels, that God really does answer the prayers of those who ask, seek, and knock. Remember that we might be the answer to someone else's prayer, and that the reward for helping others is greater than anything we could ever ask for.

What do I want to ask God for at this time in my life? Who is in need of my help? How is what I am asking for leading me to help others?

Zeki Safir and His Hungry Robe

(Middle East)

Zeki Safir was a wise man, one whom others turned to when they needed advice or assistance. He was also well liked and friendly, not too old and not too young. One day Zeki Safir was invited to a special dinner at the home of the most important man in town. On the day of the dinner, Zeki worked on his farm. As he did the hard work of farming, he thought ahead to the dinner he would be enjoying that evening. He looked forward to the people he would be with, to the conversations, and to the fun that the night would hold. As he began the day's work, he thought it was going to be an easy day. Unfortunately the work was harder than he expected, and Zeki got pretty dirty. Because he had worked so hard and long, he didn't have time to wash up. Zeki decided that it was better to go to the banquet in his work clothes, with soil on his hands and face, than to be late. So off he went, straight from the farm to the dinner.

At the door of the house, Zeki Safir heard laughter and talking inside. As he entered, no one really seemed to notice he was there. Usually many people would greet him, talk to him, and ask his opinion. Sometimes he even had a line of followers waiting to hear "Zeki" wisdom. This time, however, he milled about the room unnoticed, waiting and expecting to be seated near the host. The honorable Zeki Safir was very surprised when he was seated as far away as possible from the important host.

Realizing that no one would notice if he left, Zeki slipped out of the dining area and rushed home. Once there he washed his hands and face and changed into a new outfit, complete with a beautiful robe and a magnificent turban. Before leaving, he donned a wonderful new coat, the most fabulous one in the whole town. Smoothing the coat around him, he felt ready and left his home, looking very much like the Zeki Safir others would expect.

Again Zeki went to the important man's house, but this time he was received very differently. Once the servants saw Zeki Safir, they bowed and escorted him to the head table. The host stood and greeted him with a kiss. Zeki Safir was now seated right next to the host! He was given the finest wine and served before the other guests. Those seated near Zeki presented their issues to him and asked his advice.

As the meal was served, Zeki began slipping food into the sleeve of his robe. Then he began stuffing his pockets with it. Lastly, he filled the lining of his robe with dessert. Each time he fed the coat, he said, "Enjoy the food, my wonderful robe!" At first no one said anything, but it was becoming more and more obvious that their advisor and friend was acting strangely. Finally, the host asked Zeki what he was doing and why he was doing it. Zeki Safir replied, "My friend and host, I am giving due respect to the guest that you invited. Apparently you invited my robe and not me to this feast.

Earlier I arrived straight from my farm, a little dirty and in my work clothes, and at that time no one asked if I wanted so much as a drink of water. I was seated in the far corner of the room. No one even noticed when I left the banquet. I went home, cleaned up, and put on this robe. When we—the robe and I—returned to the banquet, we were given your seat of honor and treated so well. I assumed it was the robe you had invited, and that is why I fed it."

Jesus's Story (Luke 14:7-24)

Jesus used parables to challenge the people of his day, much like Zeki challenged the guests in this story. Jesus also liked a good dinner party. In one story from Luke's Gospel, Jesus is invited to a meal hosted by a leader of the Pharisees. The Pharisees were not rabbis, but they were influential community leaders. Because Jesus is beginning to have a reputation for his teaching and healings, he is invited to this important person's home. But Jesus, like Zeki, cannot ignore the hypocrisy that he experiences at the dinner party.

During dinner Jesus notices how people compete for special places at the table to indicate their importance. Zeki challenged the hypocrisy of the dinner guests by feeding his coat and pointing out that he had not changed, only people's opinion of him had changed. Jesus challenges the hypocrisy of the people at the Pharisee's party by telling them to choose the least important places at the table. Jesus tells the guests that you can always move up, but how embarrassing to be moved down!

Then Jesus makes an even more important point. He tells a parable about a banquet in which the important invited guests fail to show up. So the person throwing the party invites people that everyone overlooks—those who are considered unimportant. Jesus's point is that when you pay attention only to important or popular people, you are not doing the will of God. The people who show hospitality to the poor, the sick, and the unfortunate will be rewarded with a special seat of honor at the Great Feast when Jesus comes again.

Who am I inviting into my circle of friends and for what reasons? Who do I exclude? Do I place high value on outward appearances and social expectations? Why or why not?

The Happy Croatian

(Croatia)

The ocean was beautiful and the sky clear as the king looked over his kingdom and sighed. He should have been happy, but he wasn't. He was never happy: not when he went to the treasury to count his riches, not when he stood over the town square as all bowed before him, and not even during the many feasts he attended. The king could not understand why he was so unhappy. He had everything.

Finally the king sent for his advisors—men and women of learning, wisdom, and experience—to ask them what he should do. They listened to the king for hours, nodding and whispering to one another as he retold stories of his unhappiness. The advisors asked to be dismissed for a time to consult with one another and to create a plan for the king. As much as the king wanted an immediate response, he agreed. The advisors met for many hours trying to come up with a plan to help the king.

Days later the group of advisors met with the king, gathering around him and whispering in hushed tones. The eldest and most-respected advisor came forward. Slowly she made her way up to the king. She was so tiny he had to bend down to hear her. She told the king that in order for him to be happy he must find the happiest man in Croatia and trade shirts with him. Then, she said, the king would be happy.

The king replied, "Fine, go find him and bring him to me. But be sure it is the happiest man in Croatia that you bring me."

The advisors divided into three groups and set off in different directions, interviewing the happy people they met throughout Croatia.

The first group searched throughout the Pannonian region and returned with a young, handsome, well-dressed man. The advisors from group one told the king that this man was very, very happy. The advisors felt sure that the king would want to trade shirts with him. His garments were well made and stylish. The man walked into the king's chamber with confidence and charm. At first the king thought he had found who he was looking for. Unfortunately when the king asked him why he was happy, the man said, "Because I am the handsomest man in Croatia." The king, who was not very handsome, sent the young man away. The king clearly could not be the happiest man in Croatia just because of his looks!

The next group had searched the mountainous region and brought in a kind teacher. The teacher seemed very happy as they led him to the king. The questions the king asked were answered with thoughtfulness and intelligence. The advisors were sure the king would want to trade shirts with the teacher. All went well until the king said, "Would you like to be in charge of all the teachers in Croatia?"

At that the kind teacher puffed out his chest as he answered, "Why, yes, that would be grand!"

The king sent the teacher away, saying he wanted someone who was happy just being who they were and not because they would have power over others.

The last group brought in a man from one of the seaside region's many poor people, who swept the cobbled streets in exchange for leftovers from the taverns. The sweeper was very happy, and he answered all the king's questions perfectly. He told the king of his job sweeping in the seaside town and of the generous tavern owners who fed him regularly. The sweeper's clothes were clean, but very old and worn. This didn't bother the king, as he was excited to find someone who was happy. "Well, Sir, would you please trade your shirt for mine?" Still appearing happy, but not saying a word, the sweeper began to walk out of the king's court.

In desperation the king leapt off his throne and ran to the man. As he grabbed him from behind, the man's jacket came off in the king's hand. The happy man turned to the king, who gasped in astonishment—the man had no shirt.

Jesus's Story
(Matthew 19:16-26)

If happiness could be purchased like a possession, the king would have done just fine. Jesus knew that possessions often get in the way of happiness and can make being a disciple harder, not easier. Once a rich young man came to Jesus and asked him how he could attain eternal life. Like the king, the rich young man was not expecting the answer that he received. Jesus's answer saddened the rich young man. He discovered that true happiness was found not in the riches that he possessed but in selling everything, giving "the money to the poor," and then following Jesus (19:21). The rich young man went away very sad.

The king in the folktale thought he could be happy by having something, in this case another man's shirt. But it wasn't the man's possessions that made him happy—he didn't even have a shirt! The man was happy just because—because he did his job well (all the streets he swept were clean) and because he had enough to eat (the tavern keepers always gave him enough food for dinner). Maybe he was happy just because he didn't have a lot of stuff. The king was astonished that someone so poor could be so happy.

Jesus concludes the parable by telling the disciples that it is difficult for the rich to attain eternal happiness, but that all things are possible. As the king eventually discovered, happiness is not the result of wealth, power, and possessions. Sometimes those things can even prevent us from attaining true happiness. We live in a society that is obsessed with winning and having. Jesus's message is not that we shouldn't win or have things, but that happiness is found in following Christ wholeheartedly.

Am I willing to do what it takes, even if it means not having all that I want, to follow Christ?

H·O·P·E

Pulling the Lion's Whisker

(East Africa)

"I'm going to marry Gloriosa," the boy's father said. "She is kind and will make a wonderful stepmother for you."

"No one could replace Mama. NO ONE!" Samuel yelled and ran away from his father.

But Samuel's father did marry Gloriosa, and she tried everything to make Samuel like her. However, nothing she did worked; as a matter of fact, the more

she tried, the meaner he was to her. This made Gloriosa
sad, so she decided to get help. She went to the potion
maker and asked for help.

"Please," she begged, "please make a potion that
will help Samuel like me. I very much want to be a good
stepmother."

The potion maker looked at her and said, "I will help
you, but first you must get a whisker from the lion on the
hill."

The lion on the hill was well known and much feared
by the villagers, but Gloriosa was not put off. After
thinking about it for a while, she finally came up with a
plan to get the whisker. First Gloriosa told her husband
she'd be gone a few days, next she went into the village
to purchase some supplies, and then she went to the
lion's home—a cave on the hill outside the village. The

cave sat a few yards away from some brush. Gloriosa set down the four packages she had purchased. She quickly unrolled the first package. After checking to be sure the lion was inside the cave (she heard it snoring), Gloriosa laid down its contents at the mouth of the cave. Inside the package was a large hunk of meat, and its aroma awakened the lion. Gloriosa ran back to the brush and hid behind the tall grass. The lion came out of the cave, sniffed and looked around, then ate the meat.

The next day Gloriosa did the same thing with the second bundle. This time, however, she stood in the brush. Sure enough, the lion came out, sniffed and looked around, and spotted Gloriosa. Her heart pounded, but the lion just gave her a long look and devoured the meat.

79

The following day she repeated the routine and stood in between the brush and the cave. Again the lion came out and sniffed. And again it looked around and spotted Gloriosa and stared at her. Despite her fear, Gloriosa stood her ground and patiently waited to see what would happen. As if on cue, the lion devoured the meat and returned to his den.

On the fourth day, with her final and largest bundle of meat in hand, Gloriosa stood at the mouth of the cave and placed the lion's meal at her feet. With her heart pounding and her palms sweating, she waited. The lion came out, sniffed, and looked up at the woman. As he bent down to eat his meal, Gloriosa pulled a whisker from his snout. The lion was enjoying the meat as she fled back to the village—running straight to the potion maker.

"Here!" she cried, breathlessly flinging the whisker at him, "I did it!" She recounted her story to the potion maker.

After a moment of silence, he said, "Very good, now go and be a stepmother."

"What, without my potion? But you said you'd make one!" She was visibly upset.

"No, I said I'd help." He looked at her and said, "How did you get the whisker?"

She began to tell the story again but saw he was shaking his head. She thought for a minute and said, almost as a question, "I got it by being patient."

"Yes, and by gaining trust and confidence. Now go, do the same with your stepson." The potion maker turned away, and Gloriosa went back to her husband and Samuel.

Not long after, and with a lot of patience, Gloriosa was finally able to build trust and confidence between her and Samuel. Samuel never forgot his birth mother, but he also grew to love and care for Gloriosa. Gloriosa and her husband had other children, but she always maintained a special bond with Samuel.

Jesus's Story
(1 Corinthians, chapter 13)

God calls us to love. This is the main message of Jesus's life and teachings. The early communities of faith knew this and tried to live out the call to love. They, like all of us, sometimes got caught up in personalities and disagreements and strayed from God's Law of love. Paul's First Letter to the Corinthians was in response to the problems that the new Christians encountered between one another. He wrote it to remind them of the importance and power of love.

Like the potion maker, Paul gives the Christian community good sound advice—have patience, faith, hope, and above all else, love for one another. Gloriosa had to have patience and take her time to slowly gain the trust of the lion. She took that lesson and applied it to her relationship with her stepson, which resulted in gaining his love. The potion maker's words were exactly what Gloriosa needed to hear. Paul's words of love were

P·A·T·I·E·N·C·E

exactly what the Corinthians needed to hear. They needed to be reminded of God's love for each person and of how, in turn, God wants us to love one another with the same degree of love.

When Paul ends his discourse on love, he reminds us that faith, hope, and love abide, but that the greatest of these three gifts is love. When we remember to love one another, we carry out Jesus's message. In her struggle to build a loving relationship with her stepson, Gloriosa had to be reminded that time and patience was needed to build trust and confidence between the two. The Corinthians also needed to be reminded of the impor-tance and power of love in building relationships within the Christian community. Although the word *love* is often misused, it holds special meaning for those who hear it and live it as Christians. Love gives us the power to stand courageously before any difficulty in life, to patiently solve any problem, to heal any division, to endure any suffering, to be compassionate with one another, and—in the end—to attain eternal happiness.

When was being patient with someone very difficult for me? How has patience helped me grow in my relationships with others? How can I be more patient and loving toward others?

P·A·T·I·E·N·C·E

Whose Gift?

(Jewish)

The three brothers were sad as they parted. They knew it would be seven years until they would be together again. Seven years seemed like a long time to the young men. Triplets were almost unheard of in their village. They had always been close, but they knew the time apart would be essential to their becoming men. Their parents bid them farewell, knowing their trips were important.

Luckily their parents were able to give each son a size-
able amount of money for his trip. They only asked one
thing in return——that their sons each bring back the
best gift that they could find.

Dar, the tallest, went south toward the warm seas.
Some of his time was spent studying, but most of his time
was spent wandering the seashore, deep in thought and
in search of a wonderful gift. Walking near the water's
edge, he noticed a large shell. After picking up the
shell, something different about it caught his eye. Each
time he looked into the shell he saw what was going on
in the far reaches of the earth. He knew that this was the
best gift and, placing it in his sack, he headed home.

Tivon, the fair-headed, went east. He met wise men
and women and learned to meditate and to listen to the

quiet. He also met a weaver who shared a secret with him; he showed him magical reeds. Tivon wove the reeds into a mat that swept him off the ground and flew him across the sky. He knew this was the best gift and, placing it in his sack, he headed home.

Nathan, the quietest, went west. He studied with the world's best philosophers and spent hours in prayer. He didn't think much about the gift he was supposed to get until the beginning of the seventh year. As he searched for it, many things were offered by salesmen, artists, and booksellers. None of them were what he considered the perfect gift. He continued his studies and prayers and took long walks in the countryside. One day he saw in the distance a beautiful tree with red blossoms. As he neared, he realized it was a pomegranate tree. When he got to the foot of the tree, he saw that one piece of fruit was hanging among all the blossoms. Looking at the pomegranate, he saw that it was perfect. It was the perfect color, the perfect shape, the perfect size—just perfect. He reached up to feel it, thinking maybe it was unreal. As he put his hand up, the pomegranate fell right into his open palm. At the very moment it fell, another perfect pomegranate grew from a bud. Nathan knew this was the perfect gift and, placing it in his sack, he headed home.

The triplets reached home seven years to the day that they left. It was a joyous reunion. Their parents barely recognized the young men who returned. The three brothers shared stories and reacquainted themselves. After the stories and the feasting, the father asked his sons how well they did on the search for the perfect gift. Each brother reached into his sack to share his treasure. The magic shell was brilliant in Dar's hand, and the flying mat astonished the entire family. The pomegranate only brought stares and silence that were interrupted by Dar's gasp.

"What do you see, Son?" the mother asked.

Dar, looking in the magic shell, said, "I see a princess, sick in bed, and her kingly father asking his doctors for help." He added, "They don't seem to be having any luck, and she seems very ill."

"Let's go see if we can help. Our travels and experiences should benefit others, and my mat can get us there quickly." Tivon said. All three brothers jumped on the mat and flew off.

As they arrived at the castle, the king, desperate for help, let them into the princess's chamber. Before anyone said anything, Nathan broke open the pomegranate and fed the princess. Immediately the princess sat up and color returned to her face. The king, overcome with joy, said to the brothers, "The one who helped my daughter shall be her husband, if she desires."

Dar exclaimed, "If it were not for my magic shell, we would never have known the princess was ill."

Tivon added, "If it were not for my magic mat, we would never have been able to get here in time to save her."

Nathan said little, knowing the pomegranate was essential to the princess's healing.

The king said, "Daughter, you decide, who shall it be?"

Feeling much better, she looked at each brother for a few minutes and finally said, "I choose the one with the pomegranate, if he will have me?"

Nathan answered, "Yes, but tell me and my brothers, why did you choose me?"

The princess replied, "The magic shell is unchanged, and the magic mat still flies; both are the same as when you arrived. But the pomegranate had to be broken open in order for me to live."

Jesus's Story (Luke 22:1-23)

Breaking something open means it will never be the same again. In order for the princess to get well, the pomegranate had to be opened up. The other brothers did have valid claims for saving the princess; after all, their gifts were necessary. They did discover the demise of the princess by looking in Dar's magic shell, and they did arrive in time to save her by using Tivon's magic mat. But the princess was very wise. She recognized it was the sacrifice that Nathan made by breaking open the pomegranate that saved her life.

Sacrifice is a central theme for Christians. In order for us to be saved, Christ had to be the Paschal lamb. This means that like the lambs sacrificed at Passover, Christ would be sacrificed. Christ's life was broken open on the cross, and his blood poured out for the sins of all. His death means that all humanity is saved from death and from slavery to sin.

The pomegranate, like Jesus, was perfect. Nathan made the sacrifice of breaking open his gift, not knowing if it would be received. Jesus offers himself to everyone, not knowing if he will be received. The princess wisely recognized the importance of Nathan's gift. We are called to recognize the gift of Christ's sacrifice each time we participate in the sacrament of the Eucharist. Likewise, the sacraments are gifts that transform us and help us to live out our faith.

What sacrifices am I being called to make in order to help others? How am I living out my faith?

Amor Como Sal

(Mexico)

King Pedro was such a lucky man. He ruled
over the most beautiful part of Mexico; had
a loving, strong wife; and had three kind, pretty, and
talented daughters. His *hijas* (Spanish for daughters)
were the lights of his life and brought him much joy.
In return, the three girls were devoted to their papá.
Each had a special relationship with her father, none
better than the others—just different.

One day the king went to each and asked, "Hija, how much do you love me?" He asked the oldest, Monica, first.

She answered, "Papá, I love you as much as I love sugar—especially when it is made into *pan dulce!*" She and her mamá made delicious sweet rolls that the king loved to eat on special mornings. It was one of two things the girls made without the cooks. His daughter's answer made the king very happy. He hugged Monica, gave her a pretty little locket, and went to ask the same of his next daughter.

The middle daughter, Gloria, answered his question with a big smile, "Papá, I love you as much as I love *pastel tres leches.*" The middle daughter and her mamá made a delicious cake with three types of milk. It was the king's favorite cake, and he loved eating it after a feast. He was very pleased with her answer and gave her a pretty ceramic bird.

At last the king went to his youngest daughter, beautiful brown-eyed Carolita, and asked her the question. The king always had a soft spot for his youngest child, and he waited anxiously for her reply.

"Papá," she said as she draped her skinny arms around his neck, "I love you like salt!"

Pedro stared at his daughter in disbelief. He expected a much better answer from his Carolita. The king was furious. His other daughters had bestowed such warm compliments on him. He couldn't believe his youngest daughter could be so unkind.

"Out!" he cried, "Out of my house! Salt is very ordinary; it is nothing compared to sugar and milk. I cannot have a daughter who loves me so little living here!" He pointed to the door. Even though Carolita cried and wailed, begging to be understood, the king wouldn't listen. He sent her out with one of his soldiers, instructing the soldier to kill Carolita and to return with her eyes and little finger as proof.

The poor soldier took Carolita to the jungle. Instead of killing her, he told her to flee to safety and to never return again. She appreciated his kindness but worried that he may be put to death for not fulfilling the king's wishes. "Please, take my little finger," Carolita insisted. Before he could respond, she took his sword and sliced off her finger. The soldier took it, amazed at her courage and concern for him. Before Carolita could do any more harm to herself, the soldier spotted a recently killed rabbit. He took its beautiful, yet vacant, brown eyes, hoping that his deception would fool the king.

Luckily the young princess found a hollowed-out tree and took shelter in it, tending to her finger. An old monk found her as he took his daily walk. He led her to a hermitage, where the girl did chores in exchange for shelter and food. One day a young man came to the hermitage, thinking that he too was called to become a monk. But when he met Carolita, he knew that she was the reason he had traveled to the far-off jungle. As it turned out, the young man was a prince from another part of Mexico. The two fell deeply in love and returned to the prince's castle to marry.

All the kings of Mexico were invited to the wedding, even Pedro. The princess, with her new husband, sat at a table just behind Pedro. As the food was served, special dishes were presented to Carolita's father. First, King Pedro was given a bowl of sugar. "What?" he said, "I can't eat a bowl of sugar!" The servants removed the bowl and brought in his next dish. This time he was served a plate of milk, like one you would give to a kitten. Again Pedro cried out, "Milk, I am not a child, please bring me a real meal." When the main dish was presented, Pedro began to eat greedily, but stopped and complained that the food had no flavor. The king didn't realize that Carolita had told the servants to give him the sugar and milk and that they were not to salt anything on his plate when the main dish was brought to him.

This time when he complained, Carolita walked over to his table and sweetly said, "Didn't you once say salt didn't matter?"

King Pedro was shocked, for no one knew the story of his daughter's insult. Everyone in Mexico had been told that his daughter had drowned, not that he had forced her out. "How do you know?" he asked.

"I am Carolita," she responded, showing her hand with the missing finger.

King Pedro wept, for at that moment he realized how valuable salt was and, more important, how much his youngest daughter did indeed love him. Begging for forgiveness, he promised to forever honor her and her husband.

Being the kind woman that she was, Carolita did indeed forgive him. She and her husband often visited her elderly papá, who died in Carolita's arms, holding the hand with the missing finger.

Jesus's Story
(John 18:15-27; 21:15-19)

Jesus knew a lot about being denied and sentenced to death by those he loved. Peter, one of his best friends, denied knowing him not only once, but three times. Peter denied Jesus because he thought he might get arrested just for being associated with Jesus. King Pedro also denied his daughter Carolita. He thought that she had rejected his love by saying that she loved him like salt. Carolita must have felt terrible when her father denied her and sentenced her to death. Her missing fin-ger was a constant reminder of his unkind words and evil intentions. Yet Carolita could not deny her love for her father.

Peter was heartbroken when he realized he had denied Jesus. He wept when the rooster crowed. Jesus could have chosen not to forgive Peter; after all, Jesus had warned Peter that he would deny him. Yet Jesus could not deny his love for Peter and forgave him. Likewise, Carolita forgave her father even though he had sought to harm her. Because she was able to forgive, and because her father was able to accept her forgiveness, they were able to have a relationship even to his death.

Before Jesus ascended into heaven, he chose Peter to lead his church—to "feed his sheep." Jesus questioned Peter three times, asking whether Peter loved him. Each time Peter answered yes, just like the three times Peter denied him. As Peter confessed his love for Jesus, a change took place within Peter and he was reconciled with Christ, just as King Pedro and Carolita are reconciled after they repent and confess their love for each other.

For Carolita, salt represented her love for her father because salt was essential to a meal—just as essential as her father's love was to her. Jesus also uses salt when teaching his disciples about loving and forgiving those who persecute them. In the time of Jesus, salt did not merely provide flavor for food; it was essential as a catalyst in starting the fire to cook the food. For Jesus, salt represented love, because love is the catalyst that allows Jesus's followers to forgive no matter what wrongs are done to them. Not only are we called to forgive those who deny us or harm us, we are also called to seek and accept forgiveness for the times when we do harm to others. Forgiving ourselves, however, may be the hardest part of forgiveness, but that is what Jesus asks of us.

Do I readily forgive those who have hurt me? Do I ask for and accept forgiveness from others?

"Some books immediately grab my attention. Any vivid description of the characters in stories makes me feel like I am right there with them. Vikki is sharing stories that tug at your heart and are parallels to the life of Jesus. What a breath of fresh air! In particular, her thought-provoking dialogue questions took me on a personal spiritual retreat as each chapter concluded. Great inspiration! Great book!"

Anna Scally, president, Cornerstone Media

"Coyote Meets Jesus takes good storytelling and makes it come alive on the printed page. The traditions and legends are vivid, and make the reader think. I found myself remembering the characters and their lessons long after reading them. Teens 'hang' on stories, and these are good ones."

Mike Patin, youth speaker (and amateur storyteller)

"The power of stories to touch upon some of the deepest truths of life remains unmatched. Likewise, the power of Scripture to inspire and transform us is rarely equaled. In *Coyote Meets Jesus,* Vikki Shepp has combined these two powerful tools to bring us a creative and engaging method to communicate faith to young people today."

Michael Theisen, director of youth ministry,
Diocese of Rochester, New York

"*Coyote Meets Jesus* provides an insightful integration of the stories of Jesus with folktales from throughout the world. This is a must-have resource for anyone who loves to use stories to enhance catechesis and faith-formation opportunities with people of all ages and cultures!"

Charlotte McCorquodale, PhD, Ministry Training Source

"Vikki has done a tremendous job bringing together both scriptural and cultural traditions through these engaging, masterful tales. The reader will return to read these stories again and again, as well as the insightful scriptural reflections. Just as the mark of a good story is how often it is shared, the mark of a good book like this will be how often it is shared with others."

Leigh E. Sterten, director of youth ministry, Diocese of Springfield—Cape Girardeau, Missouri, and codirector, Ministry Training Source